For the Huggers and Huggees of the world...

More Hugs!

By Dave Ross

(*Creator of* A Book of Hugs)

Thomas Y. Crowell   New York

"Four hugs a day are necessary for survival, eight are good for maintenance, and twelve for growth."

—*Dr. Virginia Satir*

Library of Congress Cataloging in Publication Data
Ross, Dave, 1949-
  More hugs!

  Summary: Cartoon drawings and captions describe
different kinds of hugs from pillow hugs to computer
hugs.
  [1. Hugging—Fiction.   2. Cartoons and fiction]
I. Title.
PZ7.R71964Mo 1984   [E]   83-46167
ISBN 0-690-04406-2
ISBN 0-690-04407-0 (lib. bdg.)

Hug History

Prehistoric hugs: Before the discovery of fire, people used hugs to keep themselves warm.

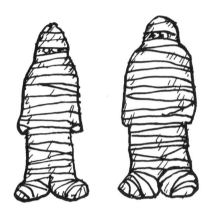

The art of hugging was nearly lost in **Ancient Egypt**. Mummies never hugged because they were all wrapped up in themselves.

The **Greeks** had a god for everything—including hugging.

The Middle Ages: Despite mechanical difficulties, knights found that hugging was the best thing to do with their arms.

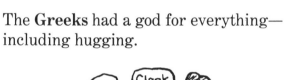

In the **Victorian Era**, hugging had to be done at arms' length.

Today: With a computer, everybody can have a Hug Program.

How to tell if someone wants a Hug

These people would all like a hug.

These people all *need* a hug but may not want one at the moment.

How to get more Hugs

Be Huggable

Wear a sign

Ask...

Some different ways of asking

Polite   Urgent   Cute

Family Portrait Hugs

Family Portrait Hugs bring everybody together.

In the studio

At the beach

On a picnic…

1.

2.

3.

Slow-Dancing Hugs—A good way to stay close
to your relatives.

Baby Hugs

Meet-the-New-Baby Hug

Itty-Bitty Hand Hug...

...When baby hugs you back

Burp-the-Baby Hug

Always be prepared
when you burp the baby.

Baby Carrier Hugs

Front Carrier Hug

Back Carrier Hug

Toddler Toe Hugs

One of the safer ways of learning how to walk

Get-Well Hugs

These hugs give instant relief…*

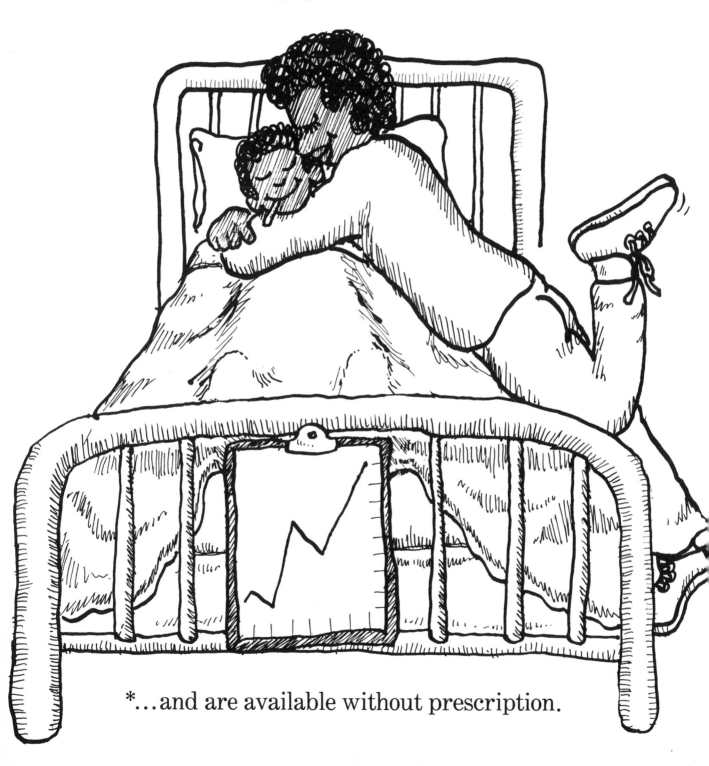

*…and are available without prescription.

Sore-Muscle Hugs
(Also known as Rub Hugs)

Back Rub

Neck Rub

Foot Rub

Rub Hugs are for people who knead people.

Hugs are good medicine for whatever ails you....

Cheer-Up Hugs help beat the blues.

Sports Hugs

Football Hugs
(Also known as Huddle Hugs)

Huddles on the field keep the team together.

Huddles in the stands help keep fans warm.

Huddles on the couch make home viewing fun.

Baseball Hug

In baseball, sometimes you get to hug the *other* team.

Basketball Hug

Ski-Lift Hugs

(Otherwise known as Hanging On for Dear Life)

These hugs are good all the way uphill.

Sled and Toboggan Hugs

These hugs are good all the way downhill.

Rug-Wrestle Hugs

(An indoor sport for the whole family)

Rug-Wrestling Rules
1. Be careful of furniture.
2. Stop tickling when asked.
3. Running starts not allowed.

Cuddles, Snuggles, & Nuzzles

Cuddles are long-lasting hugs.

Sometimes cuddlers' arms
fall asleep.

Sometimes cuddlers
fall asleep.

Snuggles

Snuggles are best at bedtime.

Nuzzles

Nuzzling is done with cheeks, chins, and noses.

Caution: An unshaven nuzzler can give you whisker burn.

(Dogs are good at giving muzzle nuzzles.)

Surprise Hugs

Ambush Hug*

*Not recommended for huggees with weak nerves

Guess-Who Hug

Gotcha Hug

(Hugger grabs huggee's ribs and says, *Gotcha!*)

It's not a good idea to gotcha-hug someone carrying food or paint supplies.

Risky Hugs

Boa Constrictor Hug

Avoid getting too tied up with a friendly boa constrictor.

Poison Ivy Hug

Stray-Kitty Hug

Hugs Risky to the Huggee

Sunburn Hug

Back-Slapping Bear Hug

Hugs Risky to Hugger and Huggee…

The Flying Zeppelin Brothers Hug*

*Should not be attempted by beginners

All-By-Yourself Hugs

Stuffed-Animal Hug

Stuffed-Animal Hugs
can get you through a stormy night.

Pillow Hugs

It's always good to sleep late with a Pillow Hug.

Self Hugs

(For Huggers without Huggees)

Poor-Me Hug

Headache Hug

(For the end of a long school day)

Fake Hug

(As seen from behind)

I-Like-Myself Hug

Hug Records

The **longest hugs** are between barnacles. These shellfish spend most of their lives glued to one another.

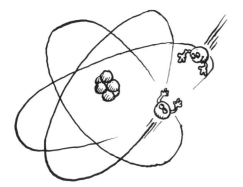

The **shortest hugs** are between subatomic particles—they have only one quadrillionth (.000000000000001) of a second to get together.

The **slowest huggers** are snails. It takes them a long time to come out of their shells.

The **fastest hugs**: With a computer you can get a hug in record time.